Willa Dean's
Cloud Dreams

Little Wings
1

Willa Bean's
Cloud Dreams

by Cecilia Galante
illustrated by Kristi Valiant

A STEPPING STONE BOOK™

Random House New York

For Sophia, my little love —C.G.

For my Ciana, may you soar
on wings. (Isaiah 40:31) —K.V.

Text copyright © 2011 by Cecilia Galante
Cover art and interior illustrations copyright © 2011 by Kristi Valiant

Visit us on the Web!
SteppingStonesBooks.com
randomhouse.com/kids

Educators and librarians, for a variety of teaching tools, visit us at
randomhouse.com/teachers

Library of Congress Cataloging-in-Publication Data
Galante, Cecilia.
Willa Bean's cloud dreams / by Cecilia Galante ; illustrated by Kristi Valiant.
p. cm. — (Little wings ; #1)
"A Stepping Stone book."
Summary: Willa Bean, who wants to master flying before starting school at Cupid Academy, celebrates her unconventional looks and unique personality, but struggles to accept that cupids learn how to fly at different times.
ISBN 978-0-375-86947-1 (pbk.) — ISBN 978-0-375-96947-8 (lib. bdg.) —
ISBN 978-0-375-98352-8 (ebook)
[1. Individuality—Fiction. 2. Flight—Fiction. 3. Schools—Fiction.
4. Cupid (Roman deity)—Fiction.] I. Valiant, Kristi, ill. II. Title.
PZ7.G12965Wi 2011 [Fic]—dc22 2011007360

Printed in the United States of America

10 9 8 7 6 5 4 3 2 1

Contents

Willa Bean's World

Willa Bean Skylight is a cupid. Cupids live in a faraway place called Nimbus, which sits just alongside the North Star, in a tiny pocket of the Milky Way. Nimbus is made up of three white stars and nine clouds, all connected by feather bridges. It has a Cupid Academy, where cupids go to school, a garden cloud, where they grow and store their food, and lots and lots of playgrounds.

Willa Bean lives on Cloud Four with her mother and father, her big sister, Ariel, and her baby brother, Louie. Cloud Four is soft and green. The air around it smells like rain and pineapples. Best of all, Willa Bean's best friend, Harper, also lives on Cloud Four, just a few cloudbumps away.

When cupids are ready, they are given special Earth tasks. That means they have to fly down to Earth to help someone who is having a hard time. Big cupids, like Willa Bean's parents, help Earth grown-ups with things like falling in love. Little cupids, like Willa Bean, help Earth kids if they feel mad, sad, or just plain stuck. Working with Earth people is the most important job a cupid has. It can be hard work, too, but there's nothing that Willa Bean would rather do.

Are you ready for a peek into Willa Bean's world? It's just a few cloudbumps away, so let's go!

Chapter 1

The Big Secret

Willa Bean sat up in bed and rubbed her eyes. The sun peeked around the edge of her window. It was morning! Finally!

She hopped out from under the covers and got dressed. There was no time to waste. Tomorrow was Willa Bean's first day at the Cupid Academy. Her best friend, Harper, would be there. So would her sister, Ariel, who was in an older cupid class.

Willa Bean picked up her silver mirror. She turned to the right. Then she turned to the left. Yesterday Ariel had told Willa Bean that she was going to stick out like a sore wing at school. This made Willa Bean a little nervous. She knew she was a very unusual-looking cupid. Other cupids had soft, straight hair, pink cheeks, and silky white wings.

Willa Bean had:

1. A crazy, curly mess of brown hair.
2. A million-bajillion freckles.
3. Bright purple wings—with silver tips!

There was not much she could do about these things. Her hair had just decided right from the beginning to grow *sideways* instead of straight down. Then it grew up, up, up, and out. Sometimes, when the wind blew just right, it looked like a gigantic, curly cotton ball!

Willa Bean's hair was *so* big and wide that she could actually hide things inside it. Sometimes, she tucked a piece of cloud treasure in the little space behind her ear. Other times, she shoved a sparklemallow or a Snoogy Bar in the very back, where the curls were the curliest. Later, when she got hungry, she pulled one of the snacks out and ate it. No one ever suspected a thing.

Willa Bean also had lots of freckles. The last time she counted, there were almost a million-bajillion of them! Mama said most of her freckles were little bits of cloud dust. This was true, since Willa Bean and Harper spent a lot of time digging for cloud treasure. They had a treasure chest buried deep on Cloud Five. It needed lots of filling. And finding treasure was a lot more important than freckles. Or clean cheeks.

Willa Bean's wings were also different-looking. But they had always looked like that—right from the start. In fact, Willa Bean could not remember a time when her wings had not been purple with silver tips. It was just how they were.

Looking different was not what bothered Willa Bean. In fact, she liked it quite a bit. She had decided that it made her a one-in-a-bajillion. And being a one-in-a-bajillion was one of the most marvelous things she could think of.

There was really only *one* thing about herself that bothered Willa Bean.

One teeny-tiny, itty-bitty, eensy-weensy secret thing.

And that was why in five more minutes, before anyone else woke up, she was going to sneak out and meet Harper at Cloud Eight.

This time, they were not going to look
for buried treasure. They were not going
to open their treasure chest and count

everything inside. They were not even going to wiggle through the cloud tunnels. Or jump in the cloud puddles until their hair got wet.

This morning, just as on all the other mornings for the past three months, Harper was going to help Willa Bean in a very special way.

She was going to try to teach Willa Bean how to get those purple wings with the silver tips of hers to behave.

Because there was no way, nohow, nope-ity, nope, nope, nope, that Willa Bean was going to start at the Cupid Academy tomorrow without being able to fly.

Chapter 2

Flying Lessons

Willa Bean skipped over the narrow feather bridge that led to Cloud Eight. Thank goodness for feather bridges. Otherwise, she wouldn't be able to go anywhere around Nimbus! She would be stuck on Cloud Four forever!

Cloud Eight was very large. It was bright pink with fat white polka dots. Lots of cupids came to Cloud Eight to play. It had high parts to it and low parts, too, which made it fun for jumping. And sliding! There were cloud puddles, and cloud tunnels, and even cloud forts on Cloud Eight.

From the bridge, Willa Bean could see Harper. She was on her hands and knees, looking for moonstones. Her blue polka-dotted glasses were sliding down her nose. The hem of her white dress was already dirty.

Harper always got to Cloud Eight before Willa Bean. But that was because she could fly there instead of walking over the bridges. Harper was lucky. Her little white wings weren't stubborn like Willa Bean's purple ones with the silver tips. They were polite little wings. Harper's wings listened when she told them to move back and forth. They paid very close attention when Harper told them to lift her off the ground. And then they *did* it.

Sometimes, Willa Bean wondered if her wings' listening parts needed to be cleaned. Or maybe they needed to be put in time-out.

Willa Bean tiptoed across the cloud. She was careful not to trip over any of the bumpy parts. It was always fun to sneak up on Harper.

"Boo!" Willa Bean yelled.

Harper screamed.

Willa Bean giggled.

"I got you again!"

"Wolla-wolla-wing-wang!" Harper's face was red. Her glasses were lopsided. "You better watch out, Willa Bean! One of these days, I'm gonna get you back and scare that crazy hair right off your head!"

"That reminds me." Willa Bean pulled a small package of sparklemallows out of the back of her hair. "It's snack time."

"Ooooh, goody!" Harper clapped her hands and wiggled her little white wings. Harper was a super-snacker. Especially when it came to sweet snacks. She had lots of sweet tooths in that mouth of hers, along with all her regular teeth.

Sparklemallows were soft pink candy with shiny blue sparkles on the outside. The inside tasted like sugar stars. Harper and Willa Bean sat down next to each other. They ate their sparklemallows slowly. Their hands got very sticky. They wiped them on the cloud until they were clean again.

"Did you find any treasure on the way over?" Harper's words were all squished together. She still had lots of sparkle-mallow in her mouth.

"Yuppers!" Willa Bean reached into her left pocket. She took out an orange moonstone, a fragment of a baby star, and a smooth white shell.

"Wizzle-dizzle-doodad!" Harper said. "You found a lot! Anything in the other pocket?"

Willa Bean reached into her right pocket. She pulled out a piece of silver chain, three blue feathers, and a length of silk string.

"Awesome!" Harper fished out half a pencil from her left pocket. It was missing an eraser. "And I found this! Let's dig up the treasure chest right now so we can put everything in it!"

Willa Bean stuffed her treasures back in her pockets. "But we have to work on my flying," she said. "Remember? Otherwise, I'll be the only one at the Cupid Academy tomorrow who doesn't know how to fly!"

Harper jumped to her feet. "Oh, that's right! Let's go!"

The two cupids walked up to the tippy-top of Cloud Eight. Willa Bean felt a little quivery inside as she looked down the sloped side. The bottom was super-soft like a pillow. If she fell, she wouldn't get hurt. But she still felt scared.

"Okay, now remember what I told you yesterday," Harper said. She bent over and put her hands on her knees. "You're gonna do it today, Willa Bean! I know it!"

Willa Bean wiggled her behind. She

shook her arms and jumped up and down. She looked over her shoulder and said, *"Boo!"* just in case her purple wings with the silver tips had fallen asleep.

"Knees bent?" Harper asked.

Willa Bean bent her knees—just a little bit, the way Harper had shown her yesterday. "Check," she said.

"Elbows back?" Harper asked.

Willa Bean pushed her elbows back. "Check."

"Chin up?"

Willa Bean lifted her chin. "Check."

"Okay now." Harper shoved her glasses up along her nose. *"Con*centrate, Willa Bean. When you push off, close your eyes and wiggle your wings super-hard. Like, harder than you've ever done in your whole entire life. Just wigglewigglewiggle the peewilly-magilly out of them."

Willa Bean took a deep breath. "Okay."

"One," Harper said. "Two! Three!"

Willa Bean rolled up on her tiptoes. She closed her eyes until she could see her little purple wings with the silver tips in her head. They were very cute. And very stubborn. *Wigglewigglewiggle.* She pushed her elbows back and lifted her chin again.

And then, with one great leap, she jumped off the very tippy-top of Cloud Eight.

For a split second, she felt the breeze on her face. The sun was there, too, soft and warm against her arms. She even heard the wind whooshing through her curls (*boing! boing!*) and Harper's voice shouting behind her. "Wiggle, Willa Bean! Wiggle with all your might!"

Willa Bean wiggled those wings. She wiggled and wiggled with all her might.

She wiggled in a way that she had never wiggled before. Her cheeks were pink and her fingers turned blue.

But it was no use. Down . . . down . . . down . . . she dropped again until at last she was lying in a heap at the soft pink bottom of Cloud Eight.

Harper flew down next to her. "You okay?"

Willa Bean spit out a piece of pink cloud and stared up at the sky. Overhead and to the right, the moon was a pale white circle. It looked as smooth as an egg. Last week, Harper told Willa Bean that her mom had taken her flying. They had gone halfway around the moon and then circled back again. Harper had even brushed the edge of a baby star with her fingertips.

When would it be Willa Bean's turn?

Willa Bean sat up and rubbed her eyes.

Her inside crying feeling was starting to push its way up from the bottom of her stomach. "No, I'm *not* okay," she said. "This flying thing is making me bonkers."

"You'll get it." Harper sat down next to her. She put an arm around Willa Bean's shoulders. "You will, Willa Bean. It just takes time."

Willa Bean squeezed her eyes tight. She had cried in front of Harper once before, after she tripped on the bridge to Cloud Six and hurt her leg. But she didn't want to cry in front of her now. In less than twenty hours, they were going to the Cupid Academy. It was *real* school, with big cupids. They were going to learn big-cupid things. Important things. Now was no time to act like a baby.

Willa Bean swallowed hard until the crying feeling inside her chest went away.

Harper patted her back. "Let's not worry about the flying right now," she said. "Let's go to Cloud Five instead and look for more treasure."

And so for the rest of the afternoon, the two little cupids dug and dug on Cloud Five until their fingernails turned bright pink with cloud dust. They found wonderful treasure—a piece of blue sea stone, three gold coins, and an old pair of wire spectacles. They dug up their treasure chest and put everything inside.

Soon the sky around them turned a light purple. Then the North Star swung its head around the Milky Way and gave them a wink. It was time to go home.

Willa Bean tucked the sparklemallow package inside her hair again and followed Harper off Cloud Five.

It had been an almost perfect after-noon.

Almost.

Chapter 3

Even Owls Have Advice

At dinner that night, Mama announced that Willa Bean had to take a shower. "And we are going to wash your hair," Mama added. "It must be nice and clean for your first day of school tomorrow, Willa Bean. No snarls." Mama raised one eyebrow, which she always did when she meant business.

Willa Bean hated showers. Especially since Mama always used fresh rainwater for them. She did not like the feel of rainwater on her skin—even if it was warm. Rainwater tingled. And it ran into her eyes. But having to take a shower *and* wash her hair was the worst. It was even worse than having to eat those icky vegetables that grew on Cloud Seven!

Hair washing involved lots of moonfoam that stung her eyes, and tons of rainwater for rinsing. Willa Bean knew she would rather eat a whole *house* full of icky vegetables than wash her hair.

"And can we please not have a Willa Bean scene this time?" Ariel asked. "The last time you got your hair washed, I almost went deaf listening to you scream and holler. It's only rainwater, Willa Bean."

Ariel was the biggest pain-in-the-wing sister ever! She thought she could treat Willa Bean like a baby just because she was older.

Willa Bean's purple wings with the silver tips fluffed up on her back. "You be quiet, Hairy Ariel! You think you're the boss of this place, but you aren't!"

Ariel tossed her long blond hair. "Don't call me Hairy Ariel!"

"Girls," Daddy said. "Remember the Cupid Rule, please."

Willa Bean thought about the Cupid Rule for a moment. It went like this:

The very best way
To spend your day
Is to try to be kind—
All the time.

The Cupid Rule sounded easy. But it wasn't. Especially when it came to big sisters.

Willa Bean stuck her tongue out at Ariel when Daddy wasn't looking.

Ariel crossed her eyes and made a face.

Baby Louie, who was sitting in his high chair next to Mama, threw a handful of peas across the room. "Da!" he yelled happily. "Da-da!"

Baby Louie was still little. He didn't have to worry about things like the Cupid Rule yet. Or pain-in-the-wing older sisters.

Sometimes, Willa Bean thought, she didn't know whether it was better to be big or little. Maybe in-between was best.

Later that night, Willa Bean sat in the middle of her bed as Mama combed out the snarls in her hair. Mama was very gentle. She did not pull or yank. But Willa Bean's eyes were still red from all the squeezing and rubbing she had done to them in the shower.

It had been an especially terrible one.

Mama had found a piece of (still wrapped) moonbubble, a rusty old key, and the leftover package of sparklemallows inside Willa Bean's hair. She had not been happy about it. In fact, she had been so unhappy about it that she had washed Willa Bean's hair not once, not twice, but three times! There had been so much rainwater and moonfoam that Willa Bean thought she was going to scream!

"I'm sorry it was such a terrible shower," Mama said softly. "But if you would stop using your hair as a storage unit, we wouldn't have to wash it over and over again."

Willa Bean sniffed. "What's a storage unit?"

"It's like a big closet," Mama explained. "We have them on Cloud Two for cupids to keep their things when they don't

have room for them anywhere else. You have pockets, Willa Bean. Lots of them. I've even sewn extra ones into your play clothes. You don't need to keep things in your hair."

"I only do it when my pockets get full,"

Willa Bean hiccuped. "And my pockets are always full. So I have to use my hair."

"You wouldn't even think about doing such a silly thing if you didn't *have* all this hair," Mama said. Willa Bean sat up straighter. She could tell Mama was getting ready for her hair-cutting speech. "If you would just let me *cut* it," Mama said, "things would be so much easier."

"No!" Willa Bean said. "Nope, nopeity, nope, nope, *nope!*" Her crying feeling was back. Only now it was starting to feel worse. She put her head down on top of her knees.

"All right," Mama said. "There's no need to get excited again. It's only hair." She pulled back the covers and poofed up the pillow. "Hop in, sweetie. You need a good night's sleep for your big day tomorrow."

Willa Bean lay down carefully so that she did not smoosh her wings. Sometimes she wondered if her wings got too smooshed from sleeping. Maybe *that* was why they didn't work.

From her bed, Willa Bean could see her brand-new uniform gown hanging in her closet. It was white with a red stripe along the bottom. It had short sleeves and a round neckline. Mama had washed and ironed it especially for tomorrow.

"Mama?" Willa Bean said.

"Yes?"

"Do I really have to wear that goofy ufinorm tomorrow?"

"U-ni-form," Mama repeated. "It's pronounced *u-ni-form*, Willa Bean, not *ufinorm*. And yes, I know you don't like it, but you have to wear your uniform tomorrow. All cupids at school have to wear them."

She gave Willa Bean an eyelash kiss, which was how all cupids kissed. "Good night, sweetheart."

Daddy came in next. He tucked the covers under Willa Bean's chin. Then he turned on both of her night-lights.

"Daddy?" Willa Bean said. "Can I ask you a question?"

"Of course." Daddy sat down on the edge of the bed. "What is it, little love?"

"Did you know how to fly when you first started school?"

"I did." Daddy nodded. "But it took me a long time to learn before that."

"How long?"

"A very long time," Daddy answered. "Weeks, I think. Maybe even a whole month. I don't think I learned how to fly until a few days before I started school."

"Well, I start school to*morrow*." Willa

Bean crossed her arms and pushed out her bottom lip. "And I *still* can't fly."

"I know." Daddy tried to smooth down one side of Willa Bean's hair. It boinged back out again anyway, even though Mama had just brushed it. "But remember, there are a lot of other things you'll be doing at school."

"But none of them will be even half as fun as flying!" Willa Bean said.

"All cupids learn how to fly at different times," Daddy said. "It will happen. You just need to take your time. Be patient."

Willa Bean fiddled with the edge of Daddy's sleeve. "Did you use one of your golden arrows today?" she asked.

Big cupids, like Daddy, used golden arrows on Earth. Golden arrows made grown-up people fall in love.

Daddy nodded. "I most certainly did."

"And did it work?" Willa Bean asked. "Did you help someone fall in love?"

Daddy leaned over and gave Willa Bean an eyelash kiss. "Yes," he said. "And before you know it, you will be using your very own orange and blue and white arrows to help little people feel happy. Sweet dreams now, Willa Bean. And don't worry so much."

But Willa Bean did worry. How couldn't she? She was going to be the only cupid at school tomorrow who didn't know how to fly!

She kicked her feet under the covers. "Dumb wings," she whispered into the dark. "Dumb, stupid wings."

"Who are you calling dumb and stupid?" came a voice from the closet.

Willa Bean sat up. "Snooze? Is that you?"

"Of course it's me. Who else would be talking from inside your closet?" A little brown owl peeked out. He flew to the end of Willa Bean's bed and fluffed his chest feathers. His wide yellow eyes were the size of half-dollars, and his head was sprinkled with little white dots.

Before cupids started school, they were each given a flying friend who taught them a little bit about Earth. Ariel had a dragonfly named Ding. Harper had a bat named Octavius. And Willa Bean had an owl named Snooze.

Snooze was an explorer. At night, he liked to fly around the world and visit different places. When he came back, he told Willa Bean about all the things he had seen. And then he slept for the rest of the day.

Willa Bean threw her covers off and

crawled to the end of her bed. "Don't worry, Snooze. I was just talking to my wings."

"You'd better be nice to those wings," Snooze said. "They're going to be doing a lot of work for you when the time comes."

"Hmph!" Willa Bean crossed her arms. "Well, right now, they're just being lazy little nincompoop wings."

"Never mind," Snooze replied. "If you want them to be nice to you, you have to be nice to them, Willa Bean. Remember that." The brown owl stretched his wings. "Well, I'm off now. Please don't forget to leave the window open for me."

"Where are you going tonight?" Willa Bean slipped out of bed. She opened the window a teeny-tiny bit.

"France again, I think," said Snooze. "Or maybe Canada. I haven't decided."

"Okay." Willa Bean put her hand over a big, fat yawn. "Well, have fun."

"*Au revoir.*" Snooze lifted a wing. "*Beaux rêves.*"

"What?" Willa Bean asked.

"*Au revoir* means *good-bye* in French," Snooze said. "And *beaux rêves* means *sweet dreams.*"

"Oh-revere." Willa Bean yawned again. "Bone reb."

Snooze rolled his eyes. "Willa Bean," he

said, "we need to work on your French."

And with a swoop of his wings, he flew into the great black night. Willa Bean watched Snooze fly. He soared and flapped, and soared some more. Soon he was only a tiny speck against the darkness.

Willa Bean got back into bed. She tried to swallow over the lump in her throat. But it hurt. Even Snooze, who was smaller than she was, could fly. And he made it look so easy.

She closed her eyes and tried to go to sleep. But that was hard, too.

Chapter 4

Think Positive!

Willa Bean tried hard the next morning to be extra sweet to her wings. She brushed them softly with her black featherbrush until they were nice and smooth. This was not an easy thing to do, since her wings were all the way behind her. But she tried it anyway. She gave her wings a little pep talk, too, using her politest voice.

"Good morning, little wings," she said. "I'm sorry I called you dumb and stupid last night. I think you are very sweet and beautiful. But it would be nice if you would start working soon. Like *today* soon. This is my first day at school, and I sort of feel like I'm going to faint. Or maybe throw up. So please stop being so stubborn and work, okay? All right, that's all I have to say for now. So, bye."

"Much better," Snooze said, flying in through the window. There was a small object inside one of his claws.

"You're back!" Willa Bean gave her owl a kiss on top of his feathery head. "Where did you go?"

"Canada after all," Snooze answered. "They speak wonderful French there. But it was very far. I'm pooped." He opened his claw and dropped the tiny item on the windowsill. It was blue and white, and very smooth. It rolled to one side.

Willa Bean picked it up. "What's this?"

"It's called a marble," Snooze answered. "They come in all different colors. Kids on Earth play with them. I found one on the sidewalk and thought you might like it."

"I love it!" Willa Bean said. "I'll put it in my treasure chest! Thanks, Snooze!"

"Willa Bean!" Mama called from downstairs. "Time for breakfast, sweetie! You don't want to be late!"

"Bye, Snooze." Willa Bean blew her pet owl a kiss. "Wish me luck!"

Snooze caught the kiss with his beak. He flapped his wings. "*Au revoir,* Willa Bean! *Bonne chance!*"

After breakfast, when Mama wasn't looking, Willa Bean slipped two peanut butter Snoogy Bars into the back of her hair. There was a chance *she* might get through the first day of school without a snack.

But Harper? Nope, nope-ity, nope, nope, nope.

Mama and Baby Louie walked Willa Bean to the cloudstop on Cloud Four. Willa Bean stopped twice so that she could pick up a few moonstones. And again when she spotted a tiny silver buckle with little flowers carved into one side.

"Willa Bean." Mama raised one eyebrow. "You are not to pick up any more junk off the clouds. Is that clear?"

Willa Bean put the moonstones in her pocket. And then, when Mama wasn't looking, she crammed the silver buckle into her hair. "It's not junk, Mama. It's treasure."

"Well, it's germy treasure." Mama frowned. "And I don't want you walking into school today with a grimy uniform. Now, no more things off the clouds!"

"Dooby!" Baby Louie gurgled and clapped his hands.

Willa Bean made a silly face at her little brother. What was he so happy about anyway? He had a stinky diaper.

The cloudstop was packed with cupids of all different ages. Ariel was already there. She was standing with a bunch of other big cupids and swinging her long blond hair. They were shouting and laughing.

Just then, the cloudbus chugged up. Willa Bean hung back a little by Mama and Baby Louie. Harper had said she would be sitting next to a window, but Willa Bean didn't see her. Willa Bean couldn't see anyone except the older cupids.

"Come on." Mama held out her hand. "Let's get on the cloudbus and find Harper."

"I can do it by myself, Mama," Willa Bean said.

"Are you sure?" Mama pulled a piece of her hair out of Baby Louie's mouth.

Willa Bean nodded. She hoped she looked very sure of herself. "Just stay here, okay? Till I find her?"

"All right," Mama said. "You go on ahead, Willa Bean. Baby Louie and I will be right here."

"Willa Bean!" Harper leaned out of one of the cloudbus's back windows. "Willa Bean! Over here! I saved you a seat!"

"Okay, Mama!" Willa Bean yelled. "I found her! Thanks for waiting!"

Mama and Baby Louie waved good-bye as Willa Bean scrambled up onto the cloud-bus. She made her way to the back and sat down next to her best friend. Harper had new ribbons in her hair and shiny black sandals. "Wow, Harper!" Willa Bean said. "You look sensational!"

"Thanks!" said Harper. "So do you, Willa Bean. I'm so excited I could wiggle myself right out of this seat!"

Willa Bean held out the blue-and-white marble from Snooze. "Look what Snooze

brought me," she said. "It's called a marble. It's from Earth. Isn't it gorgeous?"

"I love it!" Harper whispered. She picked it up and rolled it between her fingers. "We can put it in the treasure chest after school!"

Willa Bean reached into the back of her hair and pulled out a Snoogy Bar. "I brought snacks, too," she whispered. "For later."

Harper wiggled up and down in her seat.

Snacks made her very excited.

Chapter 5

The Lovely Miss Twizzle

The Cupid Academy was on Cloud Six. It was a very big building with a gold roof. There was a wide red door in front and lots of windows.

Willa Bean and Harper were in Class A. Their teacher's name was Miss Twizzle. She had frizzy golden hair. It stuck out a little bit on the sides. And she had freckles, too! On her nose and cheeks! Just like Willa Bean!

"You have freckles!" Willa Bean pulled

on Miss Twizzle's sleeve. "Just like me!"

Miss Twizzle bent down so that she could see Willa Bean up close. "They're almost exactly like yours," she said. "How about that? And what's your name?"

"Willa Bean Skylight," Willa Bean answered. "I have a million-bajillion freckles. How many do you have?"

Miss Twizzle smiled. "I only have eight." She gave Willa Bean's nose a soft squeeze. "Lucky cupid! Now let me show you to your desk."

Miss Twizzle led Willa Bean over to a desk in the middle of the classroom. Her name was on a yellow card and taped to the front. Willa Bean stared at her teacher. "How did you know my name?" she asked. "I never even met you before."

Miss Twizzle laughed. "Your parents told me. Have a seat now, Willa Bean. We're going to start class in a few minutes."

Willa Bean slid into her seat. Harper was way up front, much closer to Miss Twizzle than she was. This did not seem very fair. Especially since Miss Twizzle and Willa Bean had the same freckles! She should definitely be seated closer to her teacher.

Just then, a cupid with bright red hair sat down in front of Willa Bean. A large bow was clipped to one side of her hair. She had smooth pink cheeks and silky white wings. Willa Bean sat forward a little. She stared and stared at that green bow. It was shiny, with a green-and-white-striped middle. She wondered what it would be like to find a piece of treasure like that on a cloud someday!

Willa Bean tapped the red-haired cupid on the shoulder.

The cupid turned around and wrinkled her nose. "Yes?"

"Where did you get your bow?" Willa Bean asked.

The cupid frowned. Her eyes looked Willa Bean all over. "My mother made it, of course. What's wrong with your hair?"

Willa Bean blinked. "Nothing's wrong with my hair. That's just the way it grows."

"But it's so . . . huge." The cupid with the red hair wrinkled her nose again. "And it's snarly, too." She tossed her head. "Anyway, we're not supposed to be talking right now. So don't ask me any more questions." And she turned around.

Willa Bean sat back in her seat and crossed her arms. Everyone knew that older cupids, like Ariel, could be rude sometimes. But she hadn't expected any unfriendly cupids in Class A!

"All right, class!" Miss Twizzle clapped her hands to get their attention. "Now that everyone is in their seats, I'd like to introduce myself. My name is Miss Twizzle."

"HELLO, MISS TWIZZLE!"

Miss Twizzle smiled. "Hello, cupids. Welcome to Class A. I think we are going to have a wonderful year together. And now that everyone knows who I am, it's your turn to tell us who you are. I'd like each of you to stand up one at a time and say your name."

Willa Bean sat very still. She paid close attention. She liked things like names. They were important. Harper went first. Willa Bean gave Harper a tiny wave as she stood up, because Harper was her best friend. Even if she did have a better seat than Willa Bean did.

After Harper came a cupid named

Raymond. Raymond had a lot of shiny things pinned to the front of his shirt. Willa Bean wiggled up and down when she saw those shiny things. She didn't know what they were exactly, but they sure looked like treasure.

After Raymond came Sebastian and Sophie, and then Lola, Hannah, Michael, and Pedro.

Finally, the cupid with the green bow stood up. She smoothed down the front of her uniform. "My name is Vivienne Josephine Scholastica Wayfarer," she said. "But all of you can just call me Vivi."

"Welcome, Vivi," said Miss Twizzle.

Vivi sat back down. She folded her hands and put them in her lap. "Thank you very much, Miss Twizzle. It's a pleasure to be here."

It was Willa Bean's turn. She jumped

up and waved at her teacher. "Hi, Miss Twizzle! You already know my name, since my parents told you. But I'll say it again in case you forgot. It's Wilhelmina Bernadina Skylight. But everyone calls me Willa Bean."

"Welcome, Willa Bean," Miss Twizzle said.

"Welcome to you, too, Miss Twizzle!"

Willa Bean waved to the rest of the class. "And welcome to everyone in the class!"

"Thank you, Willa Bean," Miss Twizzle said. "That's a wonderful welcome. You may take your seat now."

Willa Bean nodded. She liked to stand up. Especially when everyone was watching her. It was fun.

"You can take your seat now, Willa Bean," Miss Twizzle said again.

Willa Bean nodded once more.

"That means sit down." Vivi turned around and glared at Willa Bean. "In your chair."

Willa Bean sat down in her chair.

And then, when she was sure Miss Twizzle wasn't looking, she stuck out her tongue at that mean, nasty Vivi.

Chapter 6

Treasure-Plus!

After everyone was done with their names, Miss Twizzle went over the classroom rules. There were a lot of them. Four, actually:

1. Raise your hand if you have a question.
2. Keep your hands, feet, and wings to yourself.
3. Pay attention.
4. Follow directions the first time.

Rules made Willa Bean nervous. They were serious business. Most of the time, Willa Bean didn't like to be serious or business-y. She liked to have fun.

Miss Twizzle also gave everyone a writing tablet, as well as a quill pen and a pot of dark blue ink.

Quill pens and ink were to be used only in school, Miss Twizzle said.

No matter what.

They were to be kept inside the cupids' desks at all times.

No matter what.

Willa Bean had never used a real quill pen before. In fact, she had never even *held* a real quill pen before. Willa Bean stared and stared at it. The quill pen had a smooth and narrow edge. It was the color of a cloudy day, Willa Bean thought. It was one of the most beautiful things she had ever seen.

It was treasure-*plus*.

"All right, class," Miss Twizzle said. "Now we are going to practice using our quill pens. Please open your tablets to the first page and write your name."

Willa Bean watched Pedro, who was sitting in the row next to her. He dipped his quill into the inkpot. He let it drip for a little bit and then started to write.

Willa Bean did the same thing as Pedro. Dip, drip, write. But when she started to make her capital *W,* a big blob of ink plopped out of the quill. "Nope, nope-ity, nope, nope, nope!" she begged in a whispery voice. But the ink didn't listen. Instead, it made a big, messy stain on Willa Bean's paper. Now her capital *W* looked like this:

Willa Bean did not want Miss Twizzle to know that she was having trouble with her ink. And she certainly did not want Miss Twizzle to think that she couldn't write her name. She mopped up the extra ink with her fingers. Then she wiped her fingers on the bottom of her uniform. It made a cute little squiggle stain.

"Ewwww!" Vivi said, leaning over her chair. "Willa Bean just made a big mess on her skirt!"

Willa Bean looked at Vivi. "You mind your own business, meany-mouth!"

"Excuse me, cupids." Miss Twizzle turned from the chalkboard. "What seems to be the problem?"

Vivi stood up. Her green bow quivered. "Willa Bean made a mess with her ink, Miss Twizzle. And she called me a bad name."

"Wizzle-dizzle-doodad!" Harper said from across the room. "What happened, Willa Bean?"

Miss Twizzle rushed over. She knelt down to look at Willa Bean's skirt. When she saw the ink stain, she made a face as if someone had pinched her. "Oh, Willa Bean! You can't wipe your fingers on your uniform! Ink won't come out!"

"She called me a bad name, too, Miss Twizzle," Vivi said.

Miss Twizzle looked up from Willa Bean's skirt. "Is that true, Willa Bean?"

Willa Bean stared down at the floor.

"What name did you call Vivi?" Miss Twizzle asked.

Willa Bean's ears were hot. She stepped on her big toe and wiggled her purple wings with the silver tips. "A meany-mouth," she said in a not-so-loud voice.

Miss Twizzle cleared her throat. "That's not very nice, Willa Bean. And I know you are old enough now to know the Cupid Rule. Am I right?"

Willa Bean nodded.

"What is the Cupid Rule?" Miss Twizzle asked.

"The very best way to spend your day is to try to be kind, all the time," Willa Bean said. She crossed her arms. "But Vivi *is* a meany-mouth! And she's a tattletale, too!"

Miss Twizzle stood up. She tapped her fingertips together. "I'm waiting, Willa Bean."

"For what?" Willa Bean asked.

"For you to apologize." Miss Twizzle's voice was very stern. "To Vivi. For calling her two names."

Willa Bean didn't say anything. Apologies could be hard, too. Just like the Cupid

Rule. Especially when she was not even the littlest bit sorry.

Miss Twizzle tapped her fingertips a little faster. "I will give you three seconds, Willa Bean."

"Tooby-looby-skadooby!" Harper called. "Just say it, Willa Bean! You don't want to get in trouble on your first day!"

"I'm sorry," Willa Bean whispered.

"All right, then." Miss Twizzle held out her hand. "Come with me, now. We'll try to clean up the ink on your skirt."

Willa Bean took Miss Twizzle's hand. It was warm and soft.

But her inside crying feeling was back. And it was all that mean old Vivi's fault.

Chapter 7

Flying Class

Miss Twizzle used special cloudroot soap on Willa Bean's uniform. She rubbed and rubbed the ink stain. By the time she was done, it didn't look like a cute little squiggle anymore. Now it looked like a big, flat, squished squiggle.

"All right, class!" Miss Twizzle called. "That's all we're going to do with our quill pens today. Please put them inside your desks along with your inkpots. Then line up for music class."

Willa Bean went back to her desk. She stared again at her quill pen. She did not want to put it in her desk. It was too beautiful to be in the desk. It was treasure-*plus*.

Quick as a snap, Willa Bean shoved her quill pen inside her hair. She pushed it all the way in the back, where the curls were the curliest. The pen stuck out a little because it was so long. But Willa Bean squished it down. She patted her hair back into place.

And then she got in line with everyone else.

Music class was very fun. The music teacher, Mr. Sunhorn, had shiny blue wings. When he wanted to get the class's attention, he tapped on his desk with a silver stick.

Willa Bean kept her eye on that stick.

It was long and smooth. It sparkled when
the sun came through the window. The tip
of it was black. What a treasure that stick
would be!

All at once, she spied a fat pink eraser on
the floor. It was right underneath Sophie's
chair! More treasure! Willa Bean grabbed
the pink eraser. She stuffed it inside her

hair, right next to the quill pen. She and Harper would fill their treasure chest in no time as long as they kept coming back to school!

Mr. Sunhorn taught the class a song about the wind and the stars. He said they could sing the song whenever an Earth baby needed help getting to sleep. It was a nice song. Willa Bean wondered if it would work on Baby Louie. Her little brother always fussed before he went to bed.

After music class, Miss Twizzle lined the cupids back up.

"Where are we going now?" Willa Bean asked.

"To the arena," Miss Twizzle said. "It's time for everybody's favorite! Flying class!"

The other cupids cheered and jumped up and down. But Willa Bean's heart thumped inside her chest. Her hands felt cold. Her throw-up feeling was back.

"Don't worry, Willa Bean," Harper whispered. "We probably won't have to do any real flying today."

Willa Bean stared straight ahead. She wasn't so sure.

The flying teacher's name was Mr. Rightflight. He did not have much hair, and he was not very tall. But he had bright red wings that fluttered at the tips. A shiny silver whistle hung around his neck.

Mr. Rightflight blew his whistle as the cupids walked into the arena. "Welcome to flying class, cupids!" he yelled. "Let's see what you can do today!"

Willa Bean glanced over at Miss Twizzle. Her teacher was sitting on the side, watching the class. Willa Bean squeezed her eyes shut. Now even her *teacher* would know she couldn't fly!

Mr. Rightflight walked up to Raymond with the shiny treasure things all over his shirt. "What's your name, cupid?" He had a big, booming voice.

"Raymond," Raymond whispered.

"All right, Raymond!" Mr. Rightflight put a hand on Raymond's shoulder. "Stand on that red line over there and let me see how far you can fly!"

Raymond looked at Pedro and Michael and then walked over to the red line.

"Toes *on* the line!" Mr. Rightflight boomed.

Raymond put his toes on the line. He lifted his arms and raised himself up on his tiptoes. His little white wings wiggled back and forth. He grunted. But nothing happened.

"Go ahead!" Mr. Rightflight blew on his whistle. "Let's see what you can do!"

Raymond tried again. He bent and wiggled and lifted and grunted.

Still nothing.

Maybe Daddy was right, Willa Bean thought. *Maybe I* won't *be the only cupid in school who doesn't know how to fly yet! Raymond and I will be the can't-fliers! We can start our own can't-fly-yet team!*

Mr. Rightflight walked over to Raymond. "Have you flown at all yet, cupid?" His voice was not so loud now.

"Lots of times!" Raymond's voice was quivery. "I fly around at home, and in the playground on Cloud Eight, too. I don't know what's wrong."

"Hmmmm . . ." Mr. Rightflight peered at Raymond's chest. "What are those things on your shirt?"

Raymond puffed his chest out a little. "They're medals. My grandpa got them.

For doing so much good stuff on Earth. He told me that I could wear them today for my first day at school."

Willa Bean straightened up. *Medals?* Real, honest-to-goodness medals? That was the best treasure she had ever *heard* of! It was even better than a quill pen or a silver stick! It was *super-treasure-plus!*

"They're very fine medals," Mr. Right-flight said. "But they're weighing you down, Raymond. They're making you too heavy to fly. Why don't you take them off? Give them to Miss Twizzle to hold. And then we'll see if that helps."

The cupid class watched as Raymond unpinned his grandfather's medals. Willa Bean watched very, very closely. She knew it wasn't nice, but she sort of hoped Raymond would drop one of the medals. Maybe it would roll under the seats, where no one would notice. Then she could get it later, on a secret trip to the bathroom.

But Raymond didn't drop a single medal. And when he stood back on the red line again and stretched out his arms, he flew straight up into the air.

The class cheered. Miss Twizzle cheered. Raymond flew around the arena twice. He was fast. Then he came back down.

Mr. Rightflight patted him on the back. "Terrific work, Raymond! Now you can put your medals back on."

Vivi went next. She flew straight up into the air. But she tipped a little bit to one side. And then she tipped a lot to the other side. *Wibble-wobble.*

"Keep those arms out straight, Vivi!" Mr. Rightflight yelled. "Chin up in the air!"

Vivi lifted her chin. She straightened

her arms. Her tipping stopped. She flew around the arena three more times—perfectly—and then came back down.

"Excellent!" Mr. Rightflight said.

"Thank you," Vivi answered. "Usually I don't tip at all."

Pedro was next in line, and then came Sophie, Harper, Lola, and Sebastian. All of

them flew across the arena with their little
white wings, and then came back down
again.

Willa Bean was after Hannah.

And by the time Hannah was done,
Willa Bean was pretty sure she was going
to throw up.

Right after she fainted.

Chapter 8

Treasure Spells Trouble

Harper squeezed Willa Bean's hand. "It'll be okay," she whispered. "Just concentrate, Willa Bean. And *wiggle*."

"Next!" Mr. Rightflight bellowed.

Willa Bean dragged her feet as she walked to the red line. She lifted her arms and rolled up on her tiptoes. Her heart was beating like crazy. Her neck was boiling hot. The throw-up feeling was right in the back of her throat.

"Hold on just a minute, Willa Bean,"

Miss Twizzle called out from her seat.

Willa Bean lowered her arms. Did Miss Twizzle know somehow that she couldn't fly? Had her teacher decided to come to her rescue? Oh, that Miss Twizzle! What a wonderful teacher she was!

"I'd like to see you out in the hall, Willa Bean," Miss Twizzle said. "Come with me, please."

Willa Bean followed Miss Twizzle out into the hall. Miss Twizzle closed the door to the arena and turned around. "Yes, Miss Twizzle?" Willa Bean asked.

Miss Twizzle tapped her fingers together. "What do you have stuck in the back of your hair, Willa Bean?"

Willa Bean's heart had stopped beating like crazy. Now it started flip-flopping around like a grasshopper. "Nothing, Miss Twizzle," she said.

Miss Twizzle stopped tapping her fingers. "Well then, please take nothing out of your hair and put it in my hand."

Willa Bean reached into the right side of her hair. She took out the two peanut butter Snoogy Bars for Harper and her to eat later. They were soft and squishy inside the wrappers. Willa Bean put them in Miss Twizzle's hand.

Miss Twizzle blinked twice. "The other side of your hair, Willa Bean."

Willa Bean reached inside her hair again. She pulled out the small silver buckle she had found on the way to the cloudstop. She took out the fat pink eraser she had found in Mr. Sunhorn's room. She put them both in Miss Twizzle's hand.

Miss Twizzle cleared her throat. "I do believe there is one more item in there," she said.

Very slowly, Willa Bean pulled out the
quill pen. It was broken at the tip. The
feather was mashed and squooshed. She
held it out to Miss Twizzle and stared at
the floor.

Miss Twizzle's pretty mouth was set in
a straight line. "You did hear me say that
quill pens are not to leave our classroom,
didn't you, Willa Bean?"

"Yes," Willa Bean said.

"And you heard me tell everyone to put

their quill pens back inside their desks, didn't you?" Miss Twizzle went on.

Willa Bean nodded. "But I just couldn't, Miss Twizzle! My quill pen is so beautiful! It's treasure-plus! I just wanted to take it back to Cloud Five so Harper and I could put it in our treasure chest!"

"It's ruined treasure now," Miss Twizzle said quietly. "And because you didn't listen, Willa Bean, you are not going to have a quill pen like everyone else for the rest of the month."

"But what will I use to write in my tablet?" Willa Bean asked.

"A regular pencil," Miss Twizzle said. "I'm sorry, Willa Bean, but that's what happens when you don't follow the rules."

Willa Bean pushed out her bottom lip. She twirled one of her curls around her finger and looked at the floor.

Inside the arena, Mr. Rightflight's whistle screeched loudly. "Flying class is over, cupids! Great job! Next week, we start practicing with bows and arrows!"

Back in Class A, Miss Twizzle handed Willa Bean a plain old, boring yellow pencil. "Take your seat now, Willa Bean," she said.

Willa Bean's lips quivered as she looked at the pencil. It was short and yellow. It had a stubby point. It was horribly ugly. She missed her quill pen terribly, even with its bent tip and mashed feather.

Just then, Vivi turned around. "Why did you have to go out in the hall during flying class?" she whispered.

"Because Miss Twizzle had to tell me a secret," Willa Bean said.

Vivi looked down at Willa Bean's pencil. "How come you have a pencil?"

Willa Bean crossed her arms. "'Cause Miss Twizzle loves me the most. She gave it to me because I'm her favorite."

Vivi wrinkled her nose. "You are *not* her favorite. And she did not tell you a secret. You got in trouble. That's why you had to go out into the hall. And that's why you have a pencil. Cupids only get pencils when they get in trouble."

"I am not in trouble!" Willa Bean yelled.

"Are too!" Vivi said.

"Am not!"

"Are too!"

Willa Bean's inside angry feeling boiled over. And before she could stop herself, she reached out and pulled one of Vivi's wings.

Vivi screamed.

"Willa Bean!" Miss Twizzle shouted. "Let go of Vivi's wing this instant!"

Willa Bean let go of Vivi's wing. In her
hand was one of Vivi's wing feathers. It
was small and white.

Vivi snatched her feather back. She
glared at Willa Bean.

Willa Bean felt very terrible. Pulling out
wing feathers was not a nice thing to do.
Especially on the first day of school.

"That is the last straw, Willa Bean." Miss

Twizzle marched over and took Willa Bean by the hand. "You are going to have to sit up here by me for the rest of the day."

Miss Twizzle pulled out a chair and placed it next to her desk. "And I will have to inform your mother about your behavior today."

Willa Bean sat down in her new chair. She stared at the floor. She had liked it before when everyone watched as she stood up and said her name. Now she didn't like it at all. Not one bit. And her inside angry feeling had turned back into her inside crying feeling.

"Wolly-golly-doodad," Harper whispered from the front row when Miss Twizzle turned around. "Hang on, Willa Bean. The day is almost over."

Chapter 9

HOLY SHAMOLEY!

Willa Bean and Harper shared a seat again on the way home. Harper let Willa Bean sit by the window this time. Mostly because Willa Bean had gotten into so much trouble at school. Harper was super-nice that way.

"Don't worry, Willa Bean," Harper said for what must have been the millionth time. "It'll be okay."

"No, it won't." Willa Bean looked at the sky as the cloudbus chugged along. It was a watery blue color. "Miss Twizzle said she was going to tell Mama everything that happened! Mama's going to tell Daddy, and they're both going to freak out!"

"Maybe you should hide," Harper suggested. "Or run away."

"I can't!" Willa Bean said. "Mama will be waiting for me at the cloudstop!"

Harper rubbed her stomach. "I'm so hungry. Do you still have that Snoogy Bar? My stomach is doing a rumblegrumble. Maybe after I eat, I'll think of something else you can do."

Willa Bean pulled a Snoogy Bar out of her hair and gave it to Harper. The other Snoogy Bar was still there, behind Willa Bean's right ear. But Willa Bean didn't take it out. She wasn't hungry.

Harper unwrapped her Snoogy Bar. It was soft and melty. She took a big bite.

"Gee, Willa Bean," she said. "With all the stuff you carry around in your hair all day, you must feel light as a feather when you take everything out again."

Willa Bean nodded. "Really light," she said. "Like I—" Suddenly she stopped talking. "HOLY SHAMOLEY!"

Harper jumped a little. *"Holy shamoley* what?"

"IT'S LIKE WHAT MR. RIGHTFLIGHT SAID ABOUT RAYMOND'S SHINY THINGS! WHY HE COULDN'T FLY!"

Harper put both hands over her ears. "Willa Bean, you're screaming."

Willa Bean lowered her voice to a whisper-scream. "Remember how Raymond wore all of his grandpa's shiny medals today on his ufinorm? And when he tried to fly at flying class, he couldn't because the medals were too heavy? And then after Mr. Rightflight told him to take them off, he could fly!"

Harper's big eyes blinked behind her polka-dotted glasses. "Uh-huh," she said.

Willa Bean started to bounce up and down in her seat. Her curls boing-boinged along with her hopping. *Hop-hop-hop! Boing-boing-boing!* Suddenly not having a quill pen for the rest of the month didn't seem so terrible. And neither did getting in trouble with Mama and Daddy.

"I FIGURED IT OUT!" Willa Bean shouted. "WHY I CAN'T FLY! IT'S 'CAUSE I HAVE TOO MUCH STUFF IN MY POCKETS! AND IN MY HAIR, TOO! ALL THAT STUFF IS MAKING ME TOO HEAVY!"

"Are you sure?" Harper asked.

"YES!" Willa Bean yelled. "And if we go down to Cloud Eight right now, I can show you myself!"

But just then, the cloudbus pulled up to Cloud Four. From the window, Willa Bean could see Mama and Baby Louie waiting at the cloudstop. Mama did not look happy. Willa Bean hoped it was because Baby Louie was chewing on her ear.

"I'll come over later," Harper said. "After you talk to your parents. Good luck, Willa Bean."

Willa Bean got off the cloudbus. She gave Mama a big smile.

"How was your first day at school?" Mama asked.

"It was wonderful!" Willa Bean said.

Mama raised one eyebrow. "Is that so? Then why did a messenger cupid just deliver a note from a certain Miss Twizzle?"

"Miss Twizzle?" Willa Bean repeated. "Who's Miss Twizzle?"

Mama put a hand on her hip. "The

note said that you had a few difficulties at school today. Would you like to tell me about it now? Or do you want to wait until your father gets home?"

"Actually," Willa Bean said, "I don't want to do either."

Mama took her hand. "Let's go," she said.

But Willa Bean dug her feet into the cloud. She pulled her hand out of Mama's and stood there.

"Heavens!" Mama said. "What's the matter now?"

"I figured out why I can't fly!" Willa Bean said. "Just now! On the cloudbus with Harper! It's 'cause—"

"Not now, Willa Bean." Mama's voice was firm. "We need to talk about what happened at school first."

"How about this?" suggested Willa

Bean. "How about *you* go home and talk to Daddy about everything, and then the two of you can meet me on Cloud Eight and watch me fly?" She tilted her head. "And then later we can talk about everything else. How does that sound?"

Mama's eyebrow went up. "We will do no such thing. And unless you would like to find yourself in even more trouble, you will come with me. Right now."

"Dow!" Baby Louie cooed.

Slowly, Willa Bean took Mama's hand again.

And then, when Mama wasn't looking, she reached around and yanked off Baby Louie's sock.

Chapter 10

The Trouble with Parents

Willa Bean headed straight for her room when she got home. She crawled under her covers. She knew when Daddy got home, she would get into a lot of trouble. But Mama and Daddy would never find her under here.

"*Bonjour,* Willa Bean."

Willa Bean peeked out from her blankets. Even in the dark of the closet, she could make out Snooze's big yellow eyes. "*Bonjour,* Snooze," she sighed. "I'm hiding."

"I can see that," Snooze said. "From whom?"

"Mama and Daddy," Willa Bean said. "Miss Twizzle called home today because I got into a teeny-tiny, itsy-bitsy, eeny-weeny little bit of trouble at school. Mama still has to tell Daddy about it. And then I know they're both going to freak out."

Snooze settled himself on the edge of

the bed. "Do you remember the last time you got in trouble?"

Willa Bean thought. "I think it was last week, when Harper and I were playing with my night-light. Mama told us to stop and we didn't. And then Harper got zinged and had to go home."

"Exactly," Snooze replied. "And what happened afterward?"

"Mama freaked out," Willa Bean said.

"*Au contraire,* Willa Bean. She did not freak out. Your mother was very calm and collected after it happened."

"She made me clean my room!" Willa Bean said. "By myself! She never makes me clean my room by myself unless she is freaking out."

"Cleaning your room was just the price you had to pay for not listening." Snooze dipped his beak inside his wing. He fluffed his feathers. "It has nothing to do with freaking out."

"But I hate cleaning my room. It was one of the worst nights of my life." Willa Bean picked at a scab on her knee. "Well, until I found that old croissant you brought me under all my socks. From Paris. That was almost like finding treasure!"

Snooze rolled his eyes. He didn't have much patience for all the things Willa Bean thought of as treasure. "My point, Willa Bean, is that I don't think your parents will freak out this time, either. Your mother is not a freaking-out sort of person. And neither is your father. Which means there is no reason for you to be hiding under your blankets."

Just then, there was a tap on the door. Willa Bean pulled the covers back over her head.

"Willa Bean?" Daddy called. "Are you in here?"

"No." Willa Bean's voice was mufflysounding.

"We're coming in," Mama said. "And please come out from under your blankets so that we can talk like regular cupids."

Willa Bean didn't move. Not even when Daddy pulled back her covers and looked down at her. "It sounds like you had a pretty rough first day at school, little love," Daddy said.

Willa Bean heaved a great big, quivery sigh. "Yes," she said sadly. "It was not one of my best days."

"Miss Twizzle said that you seem to be having trouble following directions," said Mama.

"And keeping your temper in check," said Daddy.

"I wouldn't *have* a temper if that horrible Vivi didn't make me so boiling mad!" said Willa Bean. "She said my hair was huge! And snarly! And then she tattled on me because of the ink on my skirt!"

"The only person you should be paying attention to in class is Miss Twizzle," Daddy said. "Not Vivi or any other cupid who says something unkind about the way you look."

"I know." Willa Bean stuck her lower lip out. She yanked on a curl and thought again about the Cupid Rule. It sounded easy. But it wasn't. She thought about how much she liked being different from the other cupids, too. But being different wasn't always easy, either.

"Miss Twizzle also said that you have a wonderful personality," Mama added.

"She did?" Willa Bean folded her hands in her lap. "Did she say there was anything else wonderful about me?"

Daddy coughed. "No, Willa Bean. I think that was more than enough for today."

Just then, Willa Bean remembered her wings.

"I figured out why I can't fly!" She jumped up and down on her bed. "And if you'll take me down to Cloud Eight right now, I can show you! And then everything will be all right again!"

Mama and Daddy looked at each other. "You'll have to clean your room as soon as we get back," Mama said. "No ifs, ands, or buts."

Willa Bean stopped jumping. "What's an ifsandsorbut?"

"Never mind," Mama said, putting her arm around Willa Bean. "Let's get down to that cloud and see what you can do."

Chapter 11

Fly High, Willa Bean!

Willa Bean took six moonstones, three gold coins, and two pieces of moonbubble out of her right pocket. She gave it all to Harper.

Harper's hands were full.

Then Willa Bean removed the fat pink eraser, the blue-and-white marble, and some more moonbubble from her left pocket. She gave everything to Mama.

Mama's hands were full.

"Your hair, too," Harper said. "Don't

forget the stuff in your hair, Willa Bean!"

Willa Bean bent over and shook her head. Out fell the second Snoogy Bar, an old shoelace, and the silver buckle with the little flowers on the side.

"Stars on Mars!" Ariel said. "You're like a walking pack rat! No wonder you haven't been able to fly!"

All of a sudden, Willa Bean felt the inside crying feeling come up in her throat. And it wasn't because of what her pain-in-the-wing big sister had just said. "I don't think I want to fly if I can't keep all my treasure," she told Mama. "Finding treasure is one of the best parts about being a cupid."

"I thought you might say that," Mama said. "Which is why I brought this along for you."

She pulled a soft pouch from the sleeve

of her gown. A tiny pair of wings fluttered on the sides. They were purple with silver tips. "You can put all your treasures in this pouch when you fly," Mama said.

Mama pointed to the pouch's wings. "See? It already knows how to fly. And it will fly right next to you, Willa Bean, wherever you go. Now you don't have to carry your treasure in your pockets or your hair. It can be your very own portable treasure chest."

Willa Bean stared at the beautiful little

pouch with the purple feathers. "Where did you get it?" she whispered.

"It used to be mine," Mama said. "When I was little."

"But how?" Willa Bean asked. "You don't have purple wings with silver tips."

"Oh, I still have a few purple feathers under all these big white ones," Mama said. She gave Willa Bean a wink. "Go ahead now, sweetheart."

"Ring-a-ding-a-doodad!" Harper yelled. "Let's see how it works! Put all your treasure in it right now!"

Willa Bean smiled and hugged Mama tight. There was no one like Mama. Not in the whole entire universe. "Thank you, Mama," she said.

Everyone watched Willa Bean as she climbed up to the highest part of Cloud Eight.

"You can do it!" Harper shouted. "Con-centrate!"

"Be patient, little love!" Daddy said. "Nice and slow!"

"I've got all your treasure right here!" Mama patted Willa Bean's new pouch.

"Come on, Willa Bean!" Ariel yelled. "Go for it!"

"Courage!" Snooze called.

"Doo!" Baby Louie squealed. "Doo-da!"

Willa Bean looked at Cloud Eight spread out below her. It was very far down. And very pink. She could see the fat polka dots from where she stood. They looked like giant freckles.

Willa Bean spread her arms out wide. She rolled up on her toes. She wiggled her bright purple wings with the silver tips, and shook them out. She bent her knees and took a deep breath.

And then she flew.

She flew straight into the sky, up where the blue part met the white part. The sun was warm against her face. The breeze blew through her hair. She turned around and swooped over Mama and Daddy. She flew over Ariel and Baby Louie and Harper and Snooze.

They yelled and screamed and clapped and laughed.

Willa Bean flew straight, and she flew in wiggles. She flew up a little, and she flew down. She flew in and out, right and left, over and under, and even upside down.

She flew and flew until her wings got so tired that she couldn't possibly fly another flap.

And then, just because she could, she flew some more.